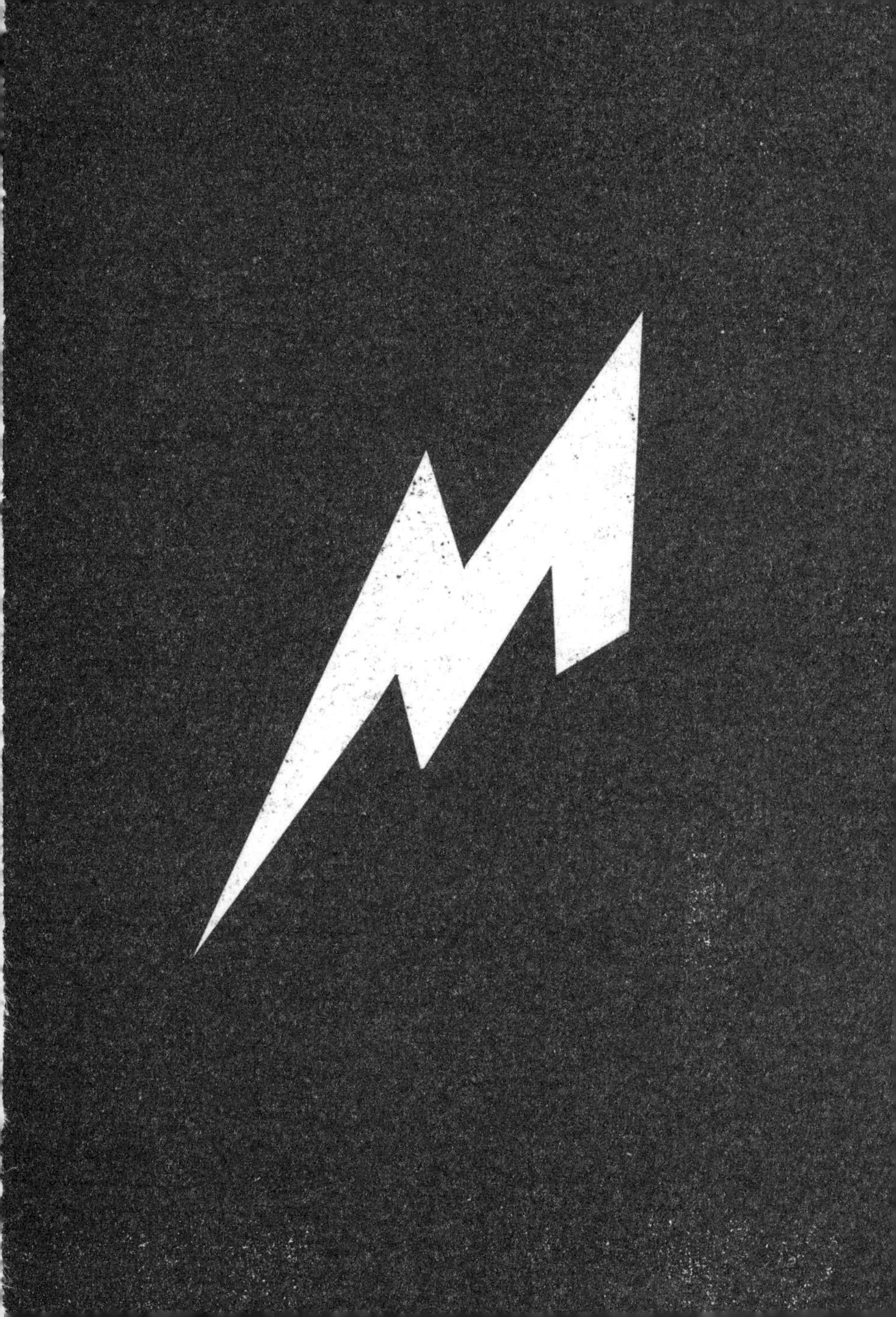

MIA MAYHEM

#10

AND THE SUPER SWITCHEROO

BY *KARA WEST*   ILLUSTRATED BY *LEEZA HERNANDEZ*

LITTLE SIMON

New York   London   Toronto   Sydney   New Delhi

LITTLE SIMON

An imprint of Simon & Schuster Children's Publishing Division
1230 Avenue of the Americas, New York, New York 10020
First Little Simon paperback edition January 2021
Copyright © 2021 by Simon & Schuster, Inc.
Also available in a Little Simon hardcover edition
All rights reserved, including the right of reproduction in whole or in part in any form.
LITTLE SIMON is a registered trademark of Simon & Schuster, Inc.,
and associated colophon is a trademark of Simon & Schuster, Inc.
For information about special discounts for bulk purchases, please contact Simon & Schuster
Special Sales at 1-866-506-1949 or business@simonandschuster.com.
The Simon & Schuster Speakers Bureau can bring authors to your live event.
For more information or to book an event contact the Simon & Schuster Speakers Bureau
at 1-866-248-3049 or visit our website at www.simonspeakers.com.
Designed by Laura Roode
Manufactured in the United States of America 1220 MTN
2 4 6 8 10 9 7 5 3 1
Library of Congress Cataloging-in-Publication Data
Names: West, Kara, author. | Hernandez, Leeza, illustrator. Title: Mia Mayhem and the super
switcheroo / by Kara West ; illustrated by Leeza Hernandez. Description: First Little Simon
paperback edition. | New York : Little Simon, 2021. | Series: [Mia Mayhem; 10] | Audience:
Ages 5–9. | Audience: Grades K–1. | Summary: After a weird storm, Mia's superpowers
are transferred to her best friend, Eddie, and she gets to train him to use them at her
secret school. Identifiers: LCCN 2020050145 (print) | LCCN 2020050146 (eBook) | ISBN
9781534484399 (paperback) | ISBN 9781534484405 (hardcover) | ISBN 9781534484412
(eBook) Subjects: CYAC: Ability—Fiction. | Superheroes—Fiction. | Best friends—Fiction.
| Friendship—Fiction. | Schools—Fiction. | African Americans—Fiction. Classification: LCC
PZ7.1.W43684 Md 2021 (print) | LCC PZ7.1.W43684 (eBook) | DDC [Fic]—dc23LC record
available at https://lccn.loc.gov/2020050145
LC eBook record available at https://lccn.loc.gov/2020050146

CONTENTS

CHAPTER 1   A STORM IS COMING   1

CHAPTER 2   STATIC SHOCK   13

CHAPTER 3   A SUPER NORMAL NIGHT   23

CHAPTER 4   A NOT-SO-NORMAL MORNING   33

CHAPTER 5   THE SUPER SWITCHEROO   43

CHAPTER 6   MEET EDDIE ELECTRIC!   57

CHAPTER 7   A SECRET PLACE   73

CHAPTER 8   SUPERHERO CRASH COURSE   85

CHAPTER 9   STILL MIA MAYHEM   99

CHAPTER 10 ANOTHER STORM   109

CHAPTER 1

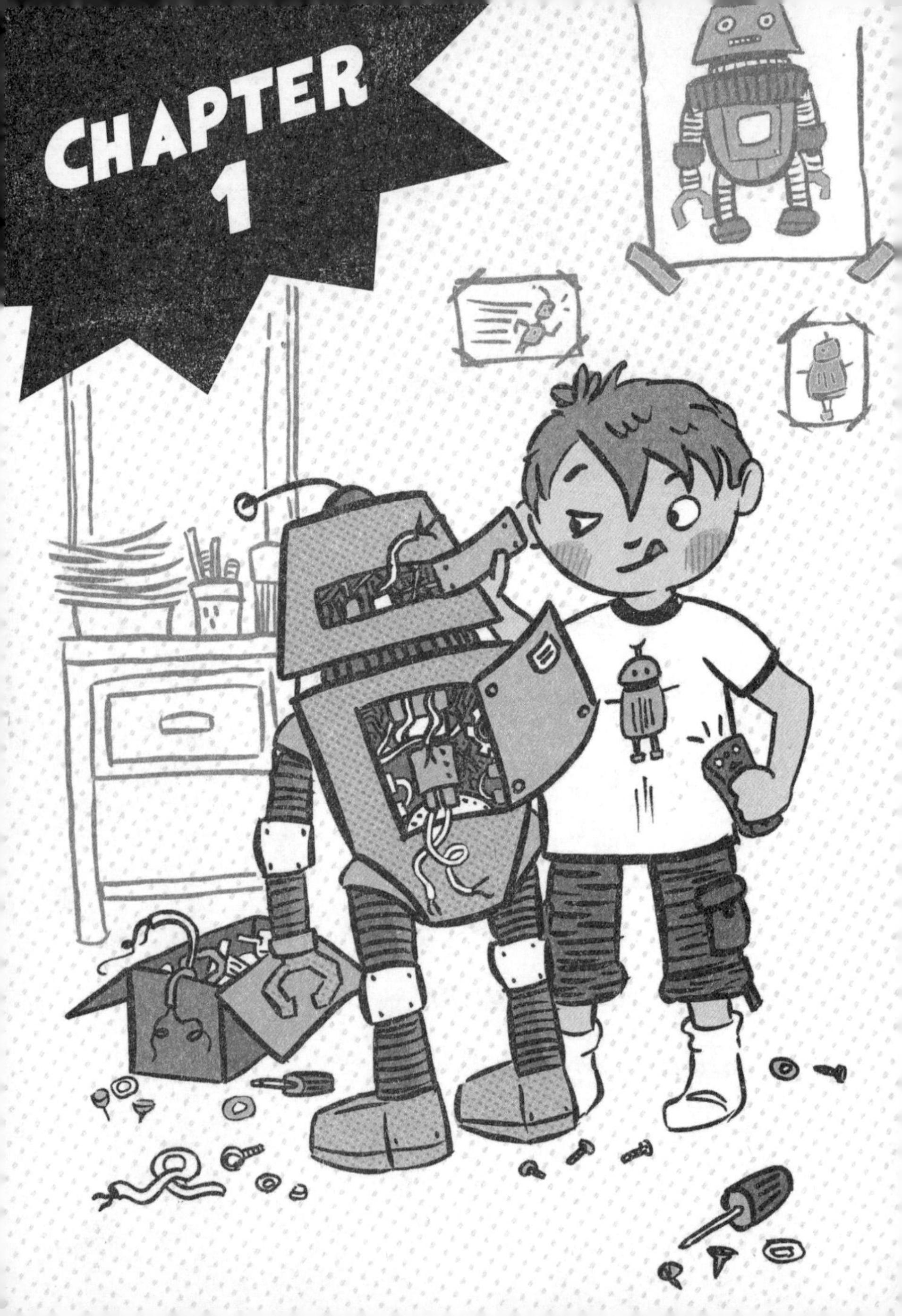

A STORM IS COMING

"Hey, can you pass me the wrench?" Eddie asked. My best friend, Eddie Stein, was busy rewiring Junior, a personal robot he built all by himself.

You see, my best friend is a genius, and making things is his idea of a perfect Saturday morning.

"No problem!" I said. "Except I think . . . the wrench is gone."

"What do you mean it's gone?" he asked with a raised brow.

I knew exactly what he was thinking: Did my powers have something to do with it?

Now, I have to admit, usually, the answer would be yes.

SPARES

As a superhero, weird things happen to me all the time. And Eddie would know. He's my only friend who knows my super-secret.

At Normal Elementary School I'm just Mia Macarooney, a regular eight-year-old kid. But after the bell rings, I quick-change into my supersuit and become Mia Mayhem!

WHOOSH!

That's right—*I. Am. A. Superhero!*

I've learned a lot in a short time, but one power I know I *don't* have is making wrenches disappear.

"I didn't do anything *super*, I promise," I said with a shrug.

Eddie looked around and then pointed to where his dog, Pax, and my cat, Chaos, were lying in a pile. After running around for hours, they had finally curled up for a nap . . . right on top of the wrench!

I leaned over, pulled it out from under Pax, and handed it to him.

I knew my best friend was a great builder, but I *was* a bit nervous. Because the last time I was with Junior, he grew three times his normal size! Luckily, with Eddie's help, I flew the giant robot out of the window before everything was destroyed.

"Okay, done!" Eddie yelled, tightening the last bolt. He pushed a couple buttons, and the robot's head lifted up. Then Junior walked toward the window, looked up at the sky, and declared in a strong voice, "STORM COMING! STORM COMING!"

Eddie and I both looked up. The sun was out, and there wasn't a single cloud in the sky.

"Aw, there must be a glitch," Eddie said, frowning.

I gave Eddie a pat on the back as he dug through his toolbox. I knew he would fix it in no time.

For now, though, I was glad it was sunny. Pax loves big storms, but Chaos always freaks out. Big-time.

As Junior's storm warning continued, both of our pets woke up.

And then . . .

Out of nowhere there was a loud crack of thunder.

Eddie and I rushed to the window.

There was nothing but sunshine.

But Junior kept repeating the same words: "STORM COMING."

And that's when we saw a lightning bolt strike down with another loud

Ever wonder how big of a mess one major scaredy-cat and one very excited dog can make?

A *giant* one.

CHAPTER 2

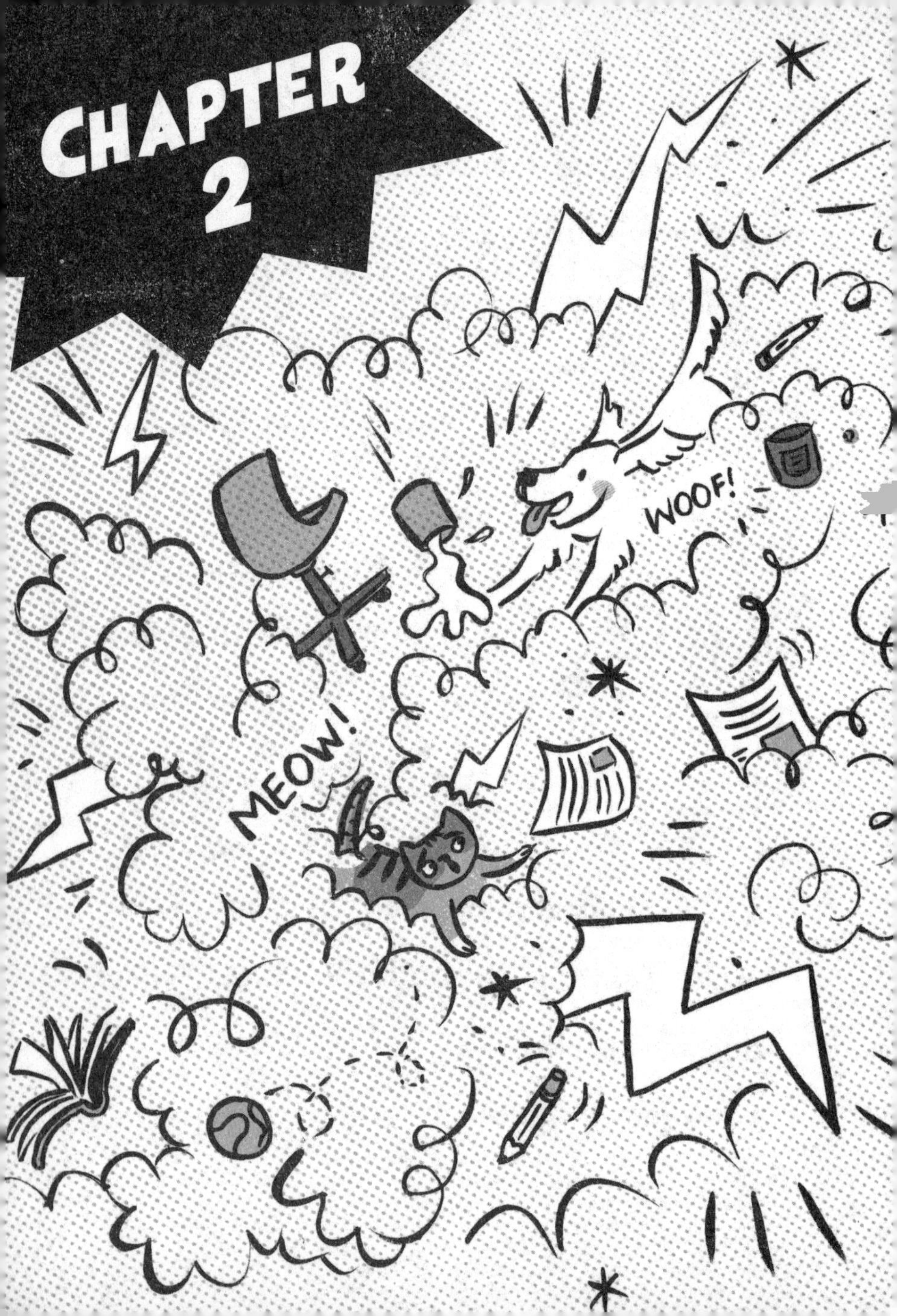
WOOF!
MEOW!

STATIC SHOCK

We didn't know what was going on outside in the sky, but inside Eddie's room, there was a dog-and-cat tornado!

Before we knew it, we were standing in a total disaster zone.

At one point, Pax finally stopped at my feet, panting with his tongue out. Chaos, on the other hand, went into hiding.

Sometimes I wonder if my cat has superpowers too. Because if she did, aside from her talent for making messes, her other secret skill would be blending into the chaos around her.

"Aw, look at this huge mess!" I cried.

There were books, clothes, and extra robot parts everywhere.

"Don't worry," Eddie replied with a smile. "Junior's weather-forecasting function may be a little wonky, but he's still good at cleaning up!"

With Junior's help (and a little bit of
my superspeed) we put the room back
together in minutes. I even found my
very unhappy cat hiding under some
pillows.

"Okay, I think I should take Chaos home now," I said, grabbing her in my arms.

Eddie agreed, so he and Pax followed Chaos and me downstairs. Eddie opened the door, and for a second, we all just stared out at the heavy rain.

Before we could stop him, Pax ran out and jumped into puddles. Chaos was still very unhappy. I held her in my arms, and Eddie and I walked out into the rain.

Eddie ran over to Pax, who was now covered in mud. We didn't want to get drenched, so Eddie and I said goodbye with our secret handshake.

But just as we were doing the elbow bump, another bolt of lightning flashed around us.

And in that moment, I felt the strangest shock. It sort of felt like the static jolt you sometimes get after doing the laundry . . . except that this tingling feeling went up and down my body.

I wanted to ask Eddie if he had felt it too. But I was interrupted by an extremely loud meow.

I looked down, and I swear, my cat was glaring at me.

I looked over at Eddie, who was now holding his big muddy dog, and we burst out laughing.

It turned out that there was no glitch in Junior after all!

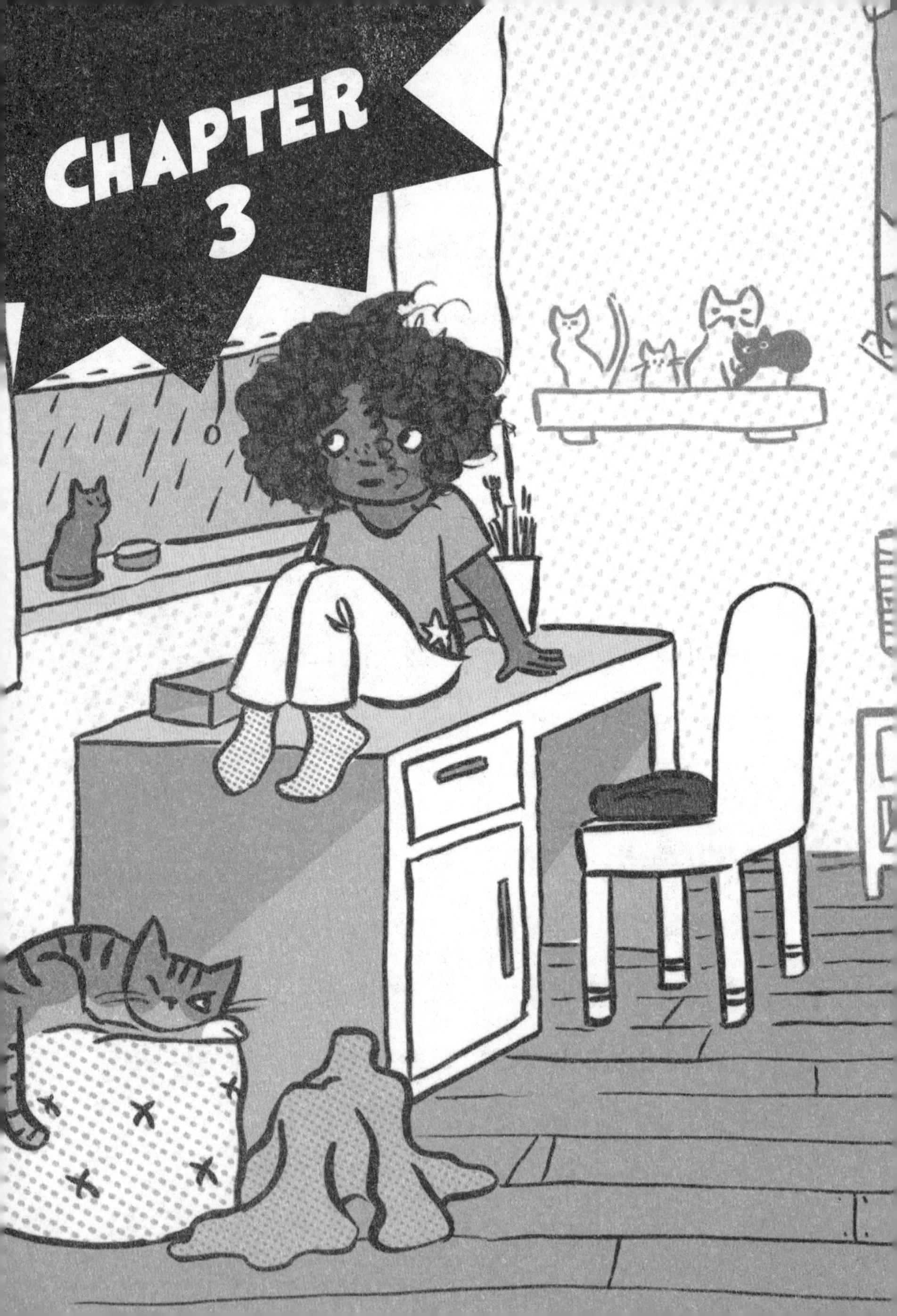
CHAPTER
3

A Super Normal Night

By the time I got home just minutes later, there was a full-on storm, with heavy, gray clouds. I'd never seen the weather change so fast!

I spent the rest of the day doing homework and reading. But every now and then, I stared out the window and watched as thick sheets of rain poured down.

Looking at the chaos happening outside, I was glad I was safe at home. I knew my cat was happy too, because soon after we got back, she dug a deep cave in my blankets.

I had a feeling Eddie was having a pretty busy night with his very happy dog. But for me, I have to say, things were pretty normal at the Macarooney house.

You'd probably expect a superhero house to be exciting all the time. I mean, it is true! We can do pretty cool stuff.

My mom is a really good flier, and my dad can talk to any animal on the planet!

But believe it or not, dinner at my house is usually very ordinary.

"Hey, honey, did you finish your math homework?" Dad asked.

"Of course," I said.

"What about your heat laser exercises?" Mom asked.

I nodded with a smile.

Okay, so maybe things *are* a little different at our dinner table.

And maybe my homework *is* a little different from other kids.

Like I said before, I still go to regular school, where I learn subjects like math and history. But every day in the afternoon, I go to a top secret super academy called the Program for In Training Superheroes! We call it the PITS. That's where I learn how to use my superpowers.

But one of the very first things I learned at the PITS was how important it was to keep your secret identity . . . um, a *secret*!

So even though we're a family of superheroes, we live a very chill, normal life. Along with doing regular homework, I also do my own chores—without powers.

That's why after we finished our dinner, I helped wash the dishes, just like any other day.

For tonight, the crazy storm outside was the only strange thing around.

Or at least that's what I thought at the time.

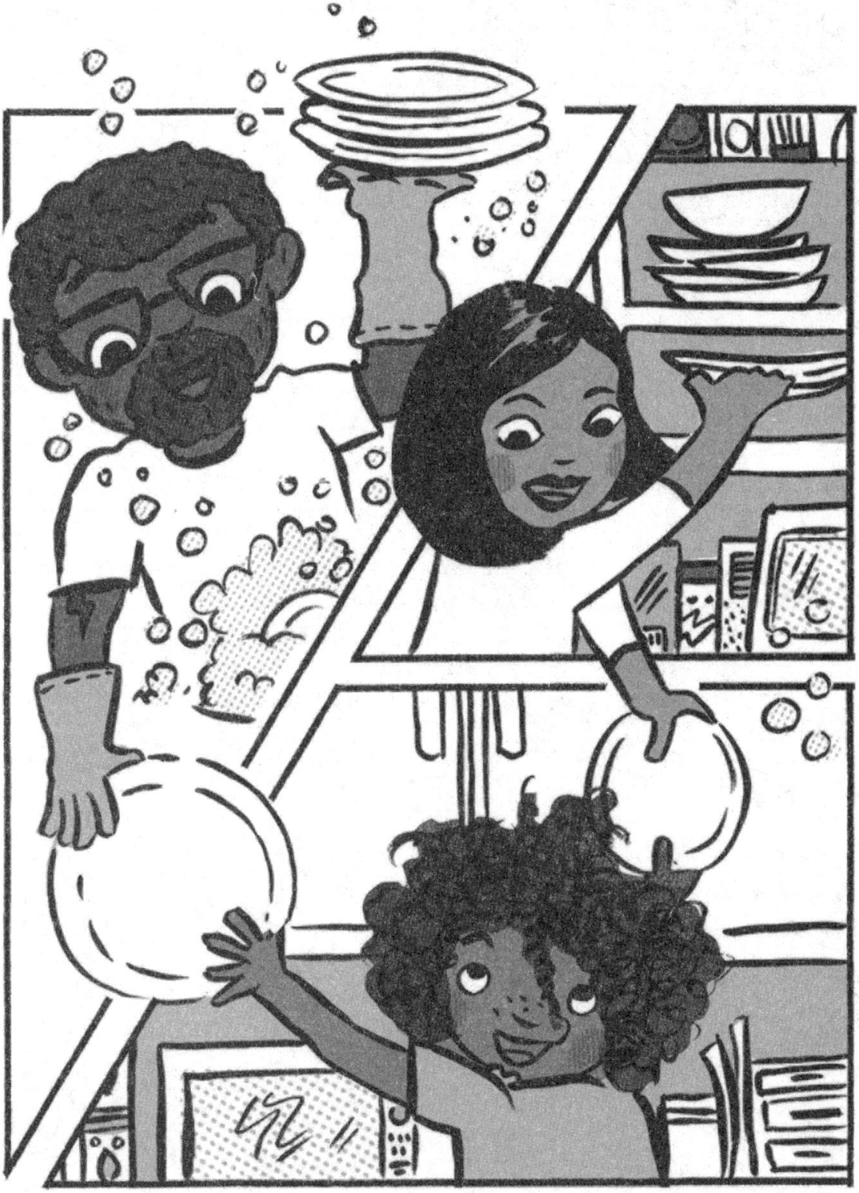

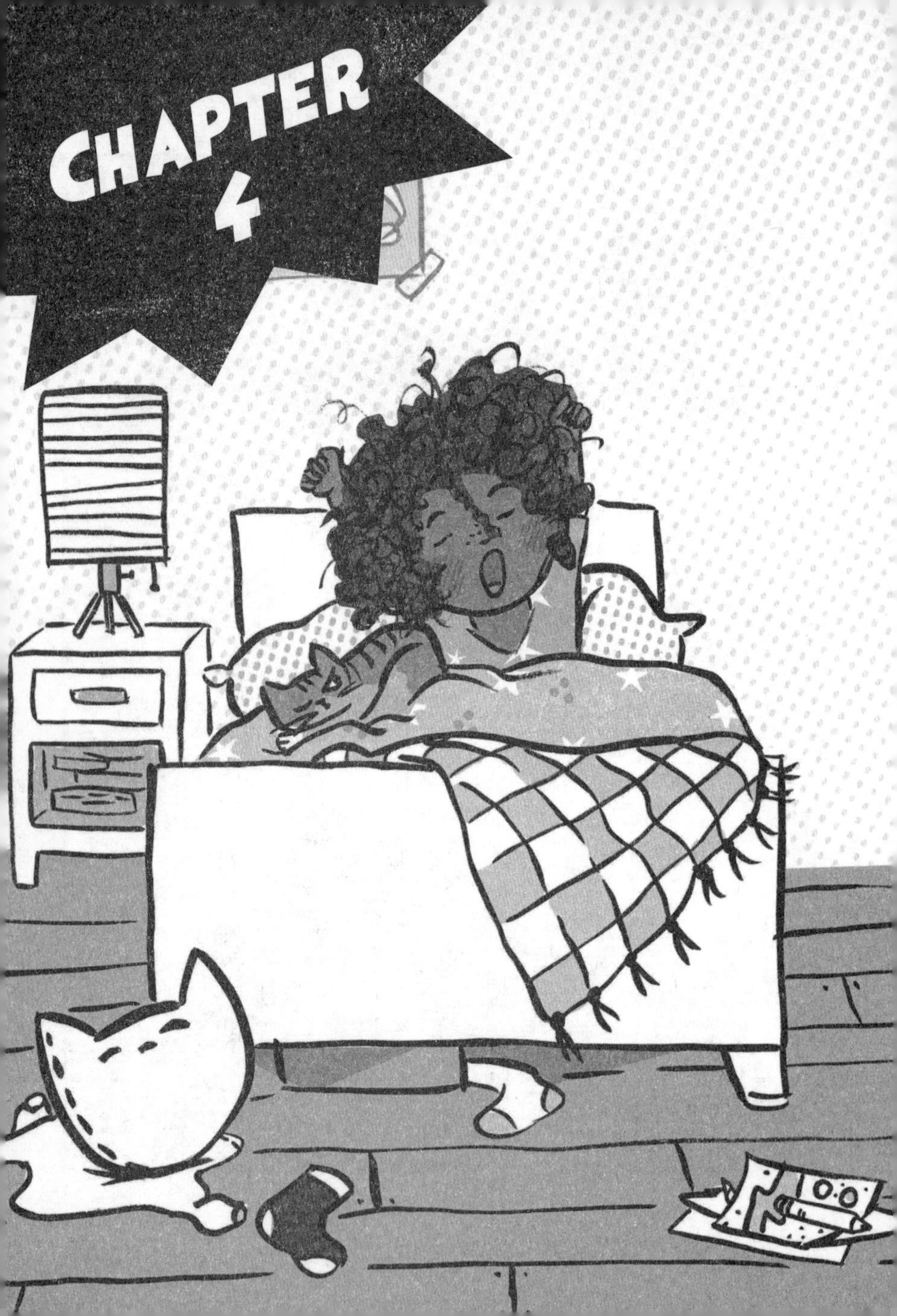
CHAPTER 4

A NOT-SO-NORMAL MORNING

When I woke up the next day, I felt it right away.

Today was going to be the *perfect* Sunday . . . to be lazy.

I quickly planned it all out in my head. I was going to wear my pajamas all day. I was going to eat waffles for breakfast. And I was going to—*knock-knock*.

I looked over at my clock. It was only seven in morning. And this knock on my bedroom door had interrupted my happy thoughts. I hopped out of bed (lazily, of course) and threw it open.

"Hey! What are you doing here?" I asked, surprised.

Here's the thing: When we hang out, it's usually at Eddie's house. His room has become a best friend hangout spot for us. So if he was at *my* house this early in the morning, that meant one of two things: something super-exciting just happened, or something was very wrong.

From the look on his face, I could tell that it was the not-good-very-wrong option.

"What's wrong?" I asked as I let him in.

"Oh, hi, Mia," he said, looking dazed.

I had never seen him so confused. So I slowly asked again what was wrong.

"I woke up, got out of bed, and at first, things were normal," he began. "But then, when I went to brush my teeth, out of nowhere, my hand moved at the speed of light!"

"Uh-huh," I said, totally unfazed.

"After that, I walked back into my room and kicked a shoe under the bed by mistake," Eddie continued. "And get this: Without thinking, I reached down and *lifted* the bed."

"Yeah?" I said, with a nod. So far, it sounded just like any normal morning I'd have.

Eddie raised his eyebrows, unsure if I was listening to him.

"Yeah, Eddie. Lifting the bed is the

quickest way to find something," I said. Then to show him, I walked over to my bed and reached down to lift it up . . .

But it wouldn't budge! Not one bit.

Finally, a light bulb went off, and my eyes grew wide.

Uh-oh. Something was *very* off.

I quickly tried to use some of my other powers.

I leaped into the air, but I couldn't fly up to the ceiling as usual.

I stared and focused hard at the wall in front of me, but no lasers came out of my eyes.

I ran laps around my room . . . but lost my breath right away.

After the toughest yet most normal workout of my life, Eddie and I looked at each other in shock.

"Mia, what is going on?" Eddie whispered with a shaky voice.

"I have no idea how," I said, "but there's been a super switcheroo!"

CHAPTER 5

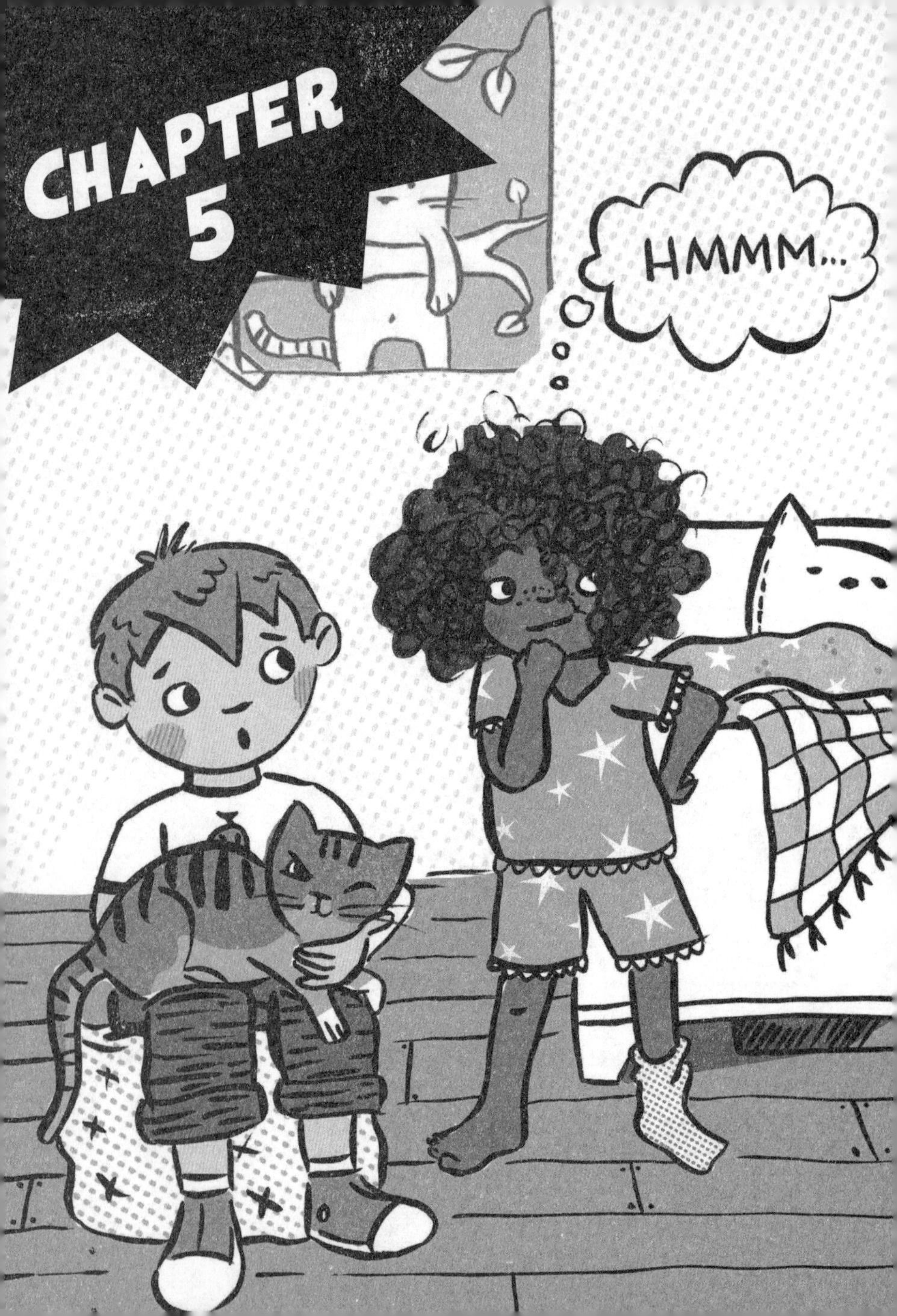
HMMM...

THE SUPER
SWITCHEROO

After trying everything, one thing was clear: All my powers were gone.

It's a funny thing, but instead of freaking out, I knew the only way to get to bottom of things was to figure out what Eddie could actually do.

It sounded like he had superspeed and superstrength, but it was time to really test him.

So I started with a strength and
speed challenge.

"Eddie, can you rearrange all the
furniture as fast as you can?"

"Okay, like that?" he asked, two seconds later. Right before my eyes, Eddie had switched things around in my room.

I couldn't believe it.

"Yes! Now can you put it back?" I asked.

"Sure thing!" Eddie exclaimed.

In the blink of an eye, my room was back to normal.

Superstrength and superspeed: check.

"Now, can you fly up and touch my ceiling fan?"

"Like this?" he asked one second later. Eddie was up by my ceiling fan.

Flying: check.

"Hmm, can you fix this broken chair using heat vision from your eyes?"

"Like that?" he asked. I looked over, and the chair looked as good as new. But then I sat down to test it out and fell right on my butt.

Laser eyebeams: sort of check.

After a handful of other things, I looked at my best friend.

"It's official," I said. "You've got all my superpowers!"

Eddie looked back at me in shock. I was surprised too.

But the funny thing is, rather than feel upset, in that moment, I realized something.

Eddie had all my powers, but he had no idea how to use them! Until we figured things out, there was only one thing I could do: teach him how to be super!

If I didn't step in, things would get dangerous. Really fast.

"What do we do now?" Eddie asked. My best friend was usually the one with the answers. But this super situation was something new.

Before I could answer, there was another knock at my door.

"Hey, Mia? I heard some noises and wanted to make sure things were okay," my mom said as she poked her head in.

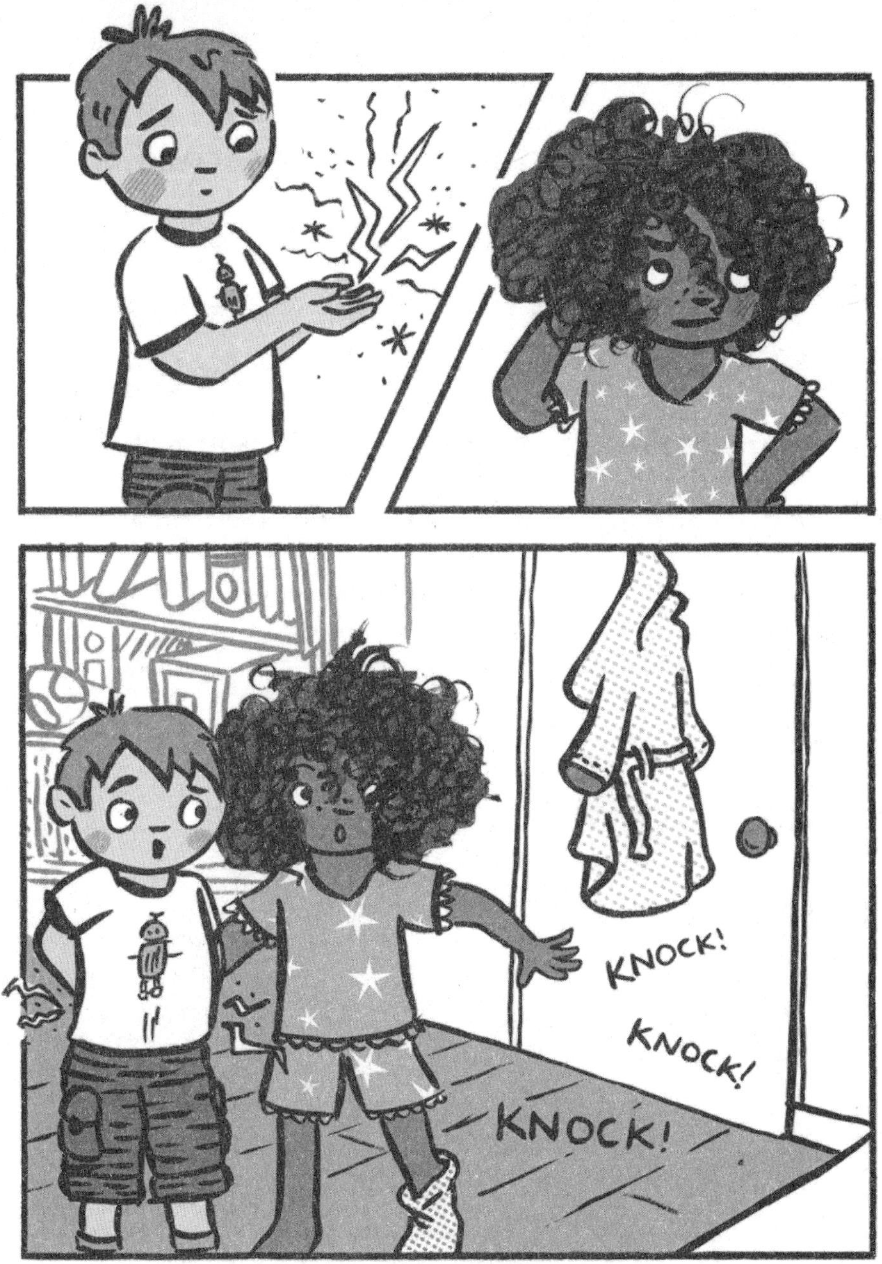
KNOCK!
KNOCK!
KNOCK!

Okay, let's stop here for a second.

Most of the time I try to solve super problems without getting grown-ups involved. Along with some of my superhero friends, like Penn Powers and Allie Oomph, Eddie and I have been able to get out of plenty of sticky situations by ourselves.

But again, this switcheroo felt different.

We needed expert superhero advice.

"Um, actually, we've got a problem," I told her.

So my mom came in and sat on my bed. Eddie and I explained the whole thing, taking turns to make sure she understood everything.

When we finished, I held my breath, unsure of what she would say.

But to my surprise, my mom just broke into a huge smile.

"I can't explain what has happened either," she said. "But the good news is that you know exactly what to do."

"I do?" I asked.

"Of course you do! You can help Eddie learn his powers!" she cried.

I smiled wide. The feeling I had in my gut was right.

"But first," she said, standing up, "Eddie needs his very own supersuit!"

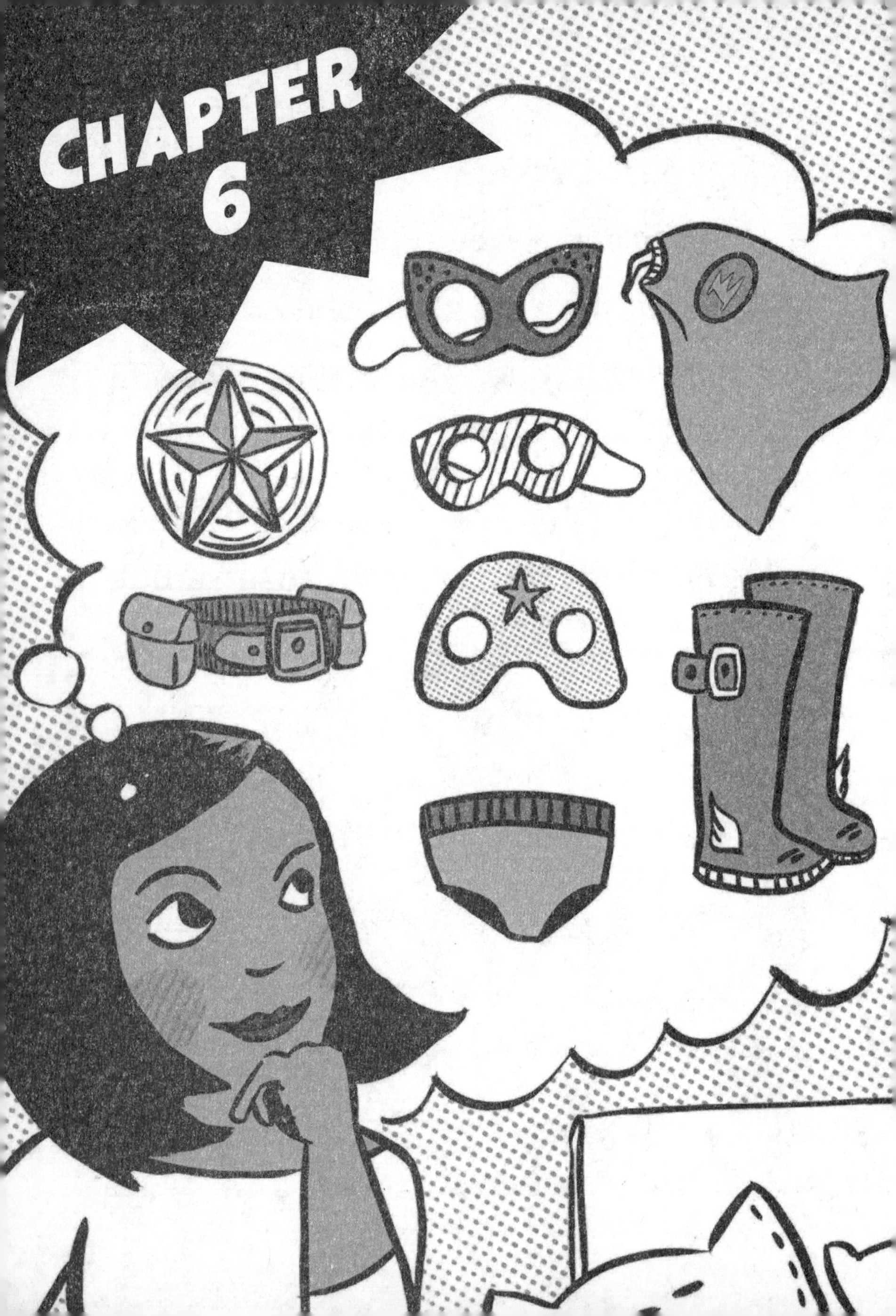
CHAPTER 6

MEET EDDIE ELECTRIC!

"A supersuit for Eddie?" I asked. "But how?"

"Believe it or not, I took some classes with Professor Stu Pendus before."

"Professor Stu Pendus made me *my* supersuit," I explained to Eddie. I knew my mom was talented, but I had *no* idea she knew how to design supersuits!

"I don't get many chances to make new suits. But let me give it a whirl!" she said excitedly.

Then she led us into her office, where she pulled out a sewing machine I'd never seen before.

"What colors do you like, Eddie?"

"I like them all, I guess . . . but yellow and blue, please!"

I smiled big. Those were my favorite colors and also the colors of *my* supersuit.

My mom nodded, pulled out some fabrics from a closet, and took Eddie's measurements. Then, using her superspeed, she sewed a supersuit for Eddie in record time.

Before we knew it, Mom held up the
finished suit.

"Yay! Try it on!" I cheered.

So Eddie ran to the bathroom (because he didn't know how to quick-change yet), and when he came back, I gasped.

"Oh, Eddie! You look SO cool!"

"Thanks! This *does* feel pretty neat," he said with a smile.

My mom had sewed an *E* on his belt, which made me think. Eddie's favorite hobby was tinkering with robots and electronics.

"Hey, Eddie! Every new superhero needs a superhero name. How's Eddie Electric?"

Eddie laughed out loud. "I love it!" he cried.

"Your suit is perfect, but it's not quite finished," I said as I ran to my room.

You see, believe it or not, all superheroes have a lucky charm. Mine is my grandma's necklace that my mom gave me.

And I had the perfect finishing touch that would complete Eddie's new look.

"You need a lucky charm!" I said as I handed him a yellow mask.

"But this is *your* mask!" Eddie said, surprised.

He was right. It *was* mine.

But at least for today, I wasn't going to need it.

Now, before we go any further, let's pause here. I need to be honest—I *am* scared to not have my powers. I *love* being super. And right now, I don't know if they'll ever come back! Even if they do, we have no idea how or when.

But here's the thing: If there's anything that I've learned through my training, it's that sometimes being a good superhero has nothing to do with your actual powers. Handling unexpected situations with the *right attitude* is more important.

Eddie has *always* been around to cheer me on. And he's also always kept my secret.

I knew this was *my* chance to be there for him . . . as just my normal self.

"Every superhero needs a *tiny* bit of good luck *and* a really good friend," I said with a wink.

So my best friend put on my mask, and we both looked at each other.

There we stood, side by side, as Eddie Electric and Mia Macarooney!

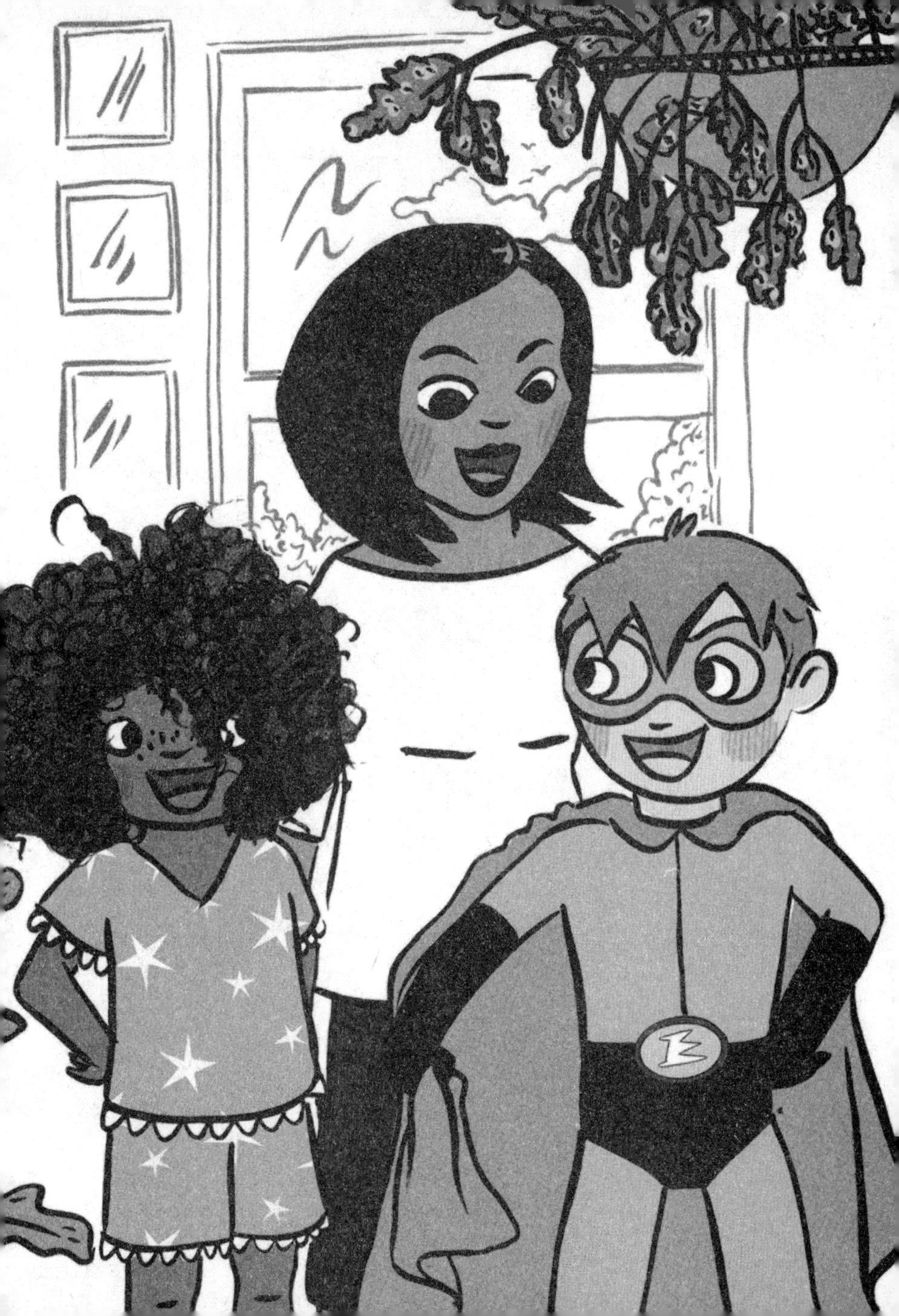

CHAPTER 7

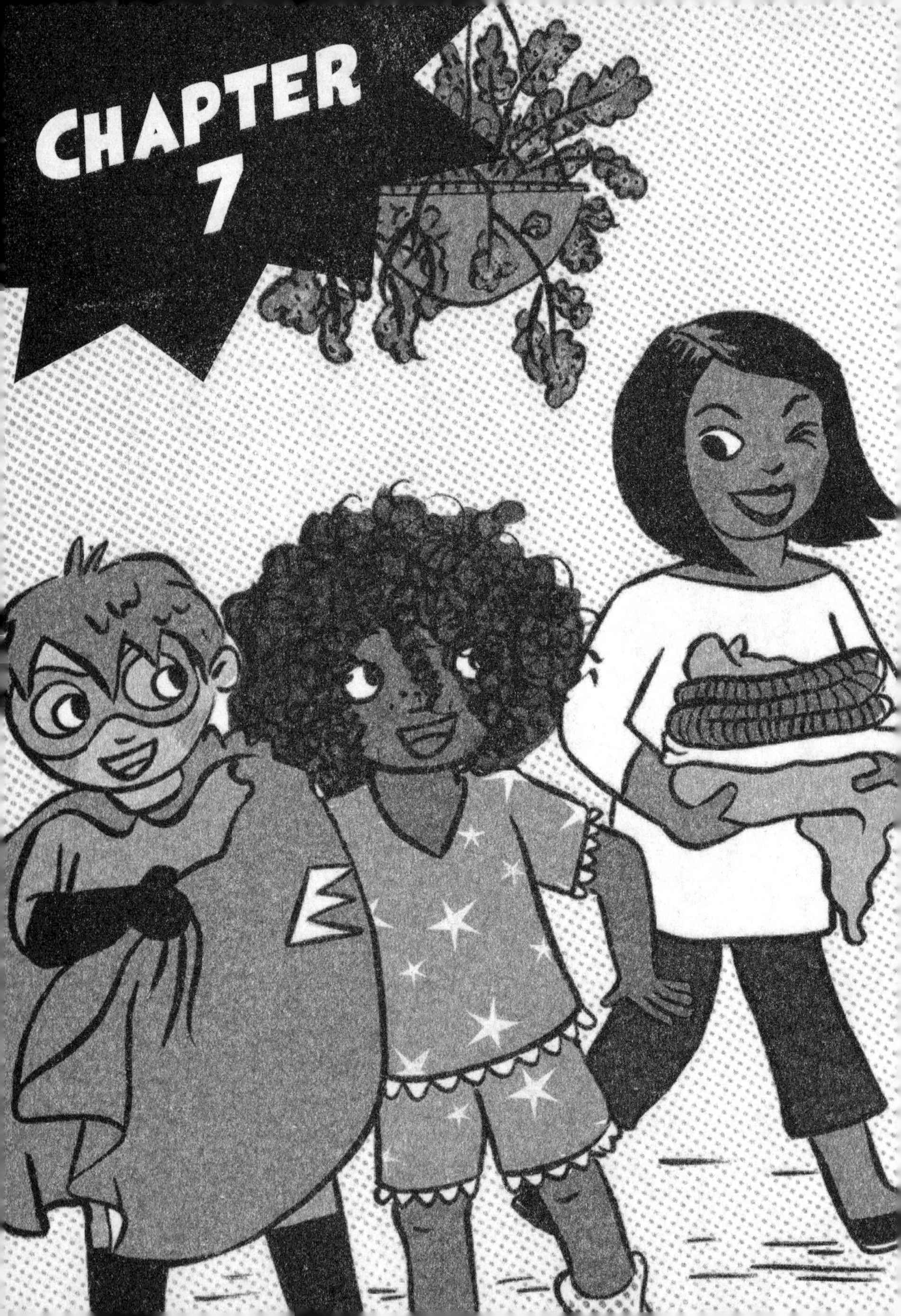

A SECRET PLACE

"You look terrific, Eddie!" my mom said.
"But the training is now in your hands,
Mia!"

She gave me wink, opened the door,
and then just like that, we were alone
again.

"Well, where do we start?" Eddie
asked.

"Okay," I said, taking a deep breath.

"At the PITS, I've learned that every superhero has to start with the basics. Even if it seems impossible at first, you'll get better if you put in the work."

"So I should start practicing?" Eddie asked as he tried to lift the sewing machine and the table it was on.

"Wait!" I cried. "Not here! We need someplace safe. Somewhere you can try out your powers without breaking things. And somewhere people can't see us."

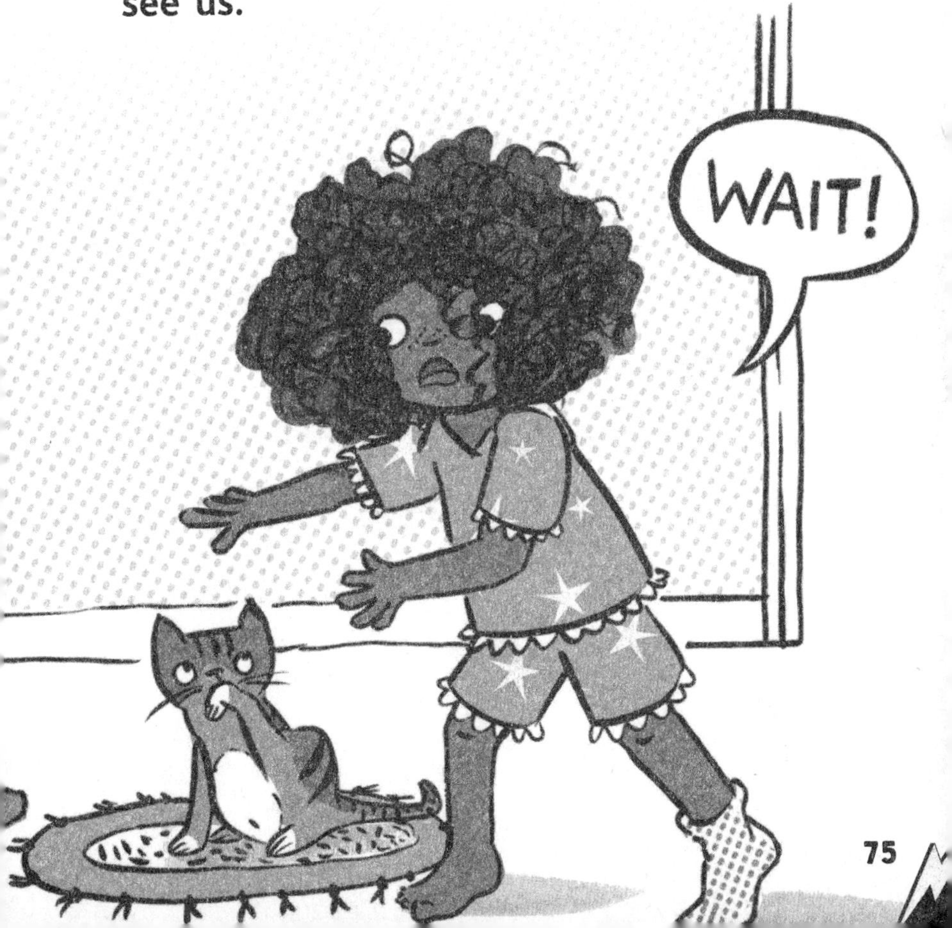
WAIT!

We paced around the room and tried to think. There had to be *some*where we could go.

But both of our yards were too small.

And the park was busy on Sundays.

Even the campgrounds would have people.

"Oh man, I'm stumped," I said after running down a list.

"Yeah, it's too bad I can't go to some school for superheroes, like you do," Eddie said.

I looked up at Eddie and gave him a
big high five.

"Wait—that's it!" I exclaimed.
"You're a genius!"

"I am?" Eddie asked. "We can't go
to school. It'll be locked."

"*Regular* school will be locked," I said with a grin. "But we can go to the PITS! Nobody will be there today, and the PITS has top-of-the-line security, so it will be perfect!"

I had no idea what to expect. Even superheroes don't go to school on Sundays! But it was the best plan we had. Eddie changed back into his normal clothes, while I changed out of my pajamas, and then we ran out the door.

Soon, we were standing in front of an abandoned warehouse that was right next to our regular school. This building looked old and boring from the outside. There was even a crooked DO NOT ENTER sign dangling on the front.

But believe it or not, *that* was the secret! I turned the slanted sign, and just like always, the face scanner popped up. I took a deep breath and then stood still.

Two seconds later the scanner buzzed green. Score! It worked!

"I can't believe I actually get to go inside with you," Eddie said in awe.

"Oh, get ready," I said, smiling. "This place is going to knock your socks off."

Then I proudly led Eddie into the PITS for the very first time.

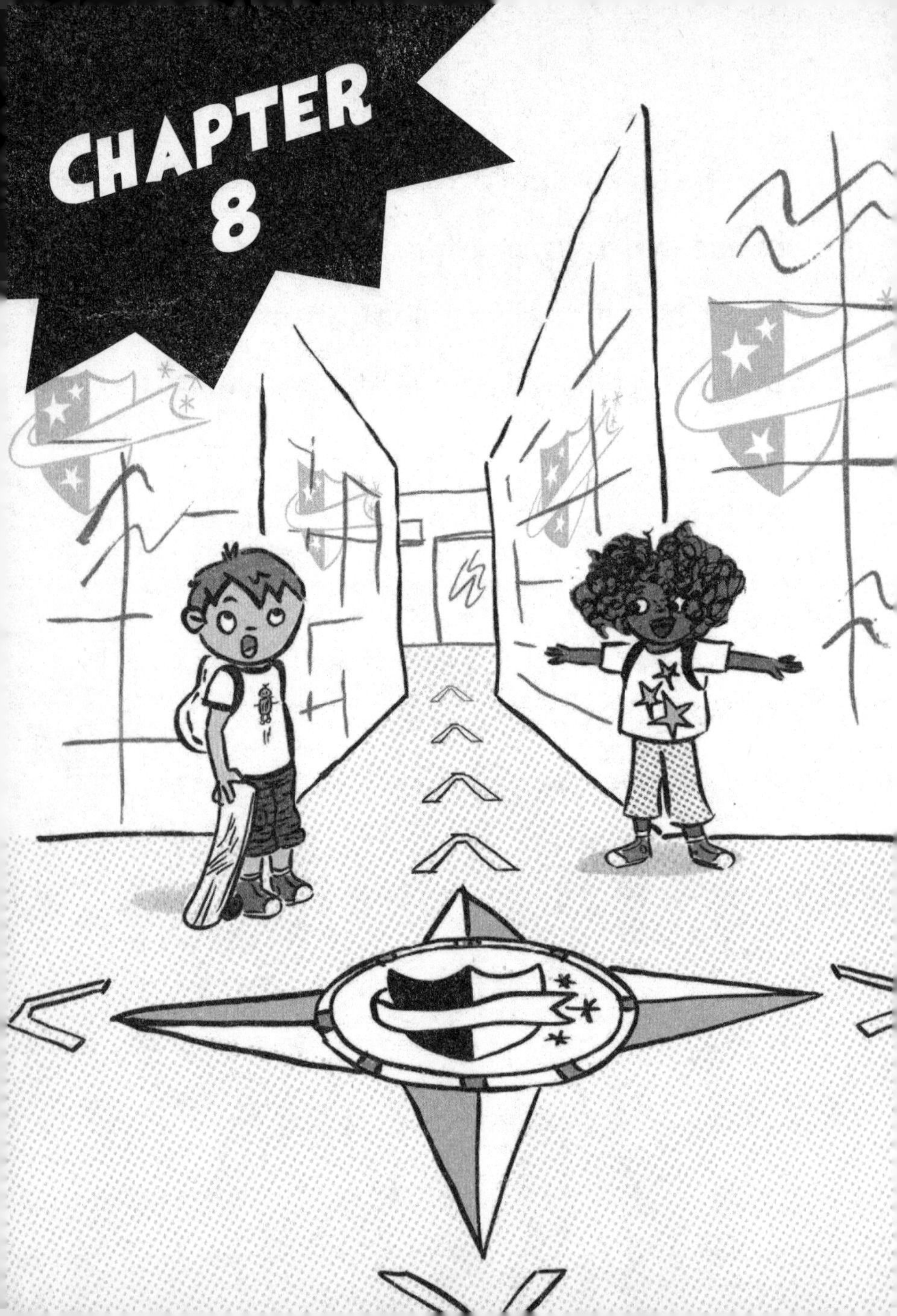
CHAPTER
8

SUPERHERO
CRASH COURSE

Eddie and I looked around the main lobby. Under our feet, a gigantic compass stretched out. It pointed to all the different parts of the training center.

Usually this place was filled with busy superheroes.

But since today was a Sunday, we were all alone. "This room is called the Compass," I told him proudly.

"Wow, this lobby is huge," Eddie whispered as he looked down each hallway.

Eddie was right. This school was huge but felt even bigger with just the two of us here. But when I looked down at the floor, I remembered something Dr. Sue Perb, our headmistress, had once told me: If you ever get lost, the Compass will always show you the way.

"Hey, Eddie!" I cried. "Come here and stand in the center of the Compass!"

He was confused, but did as I said. Then we waited, and just like Dr. Perb promised, one of the compass points lit up!

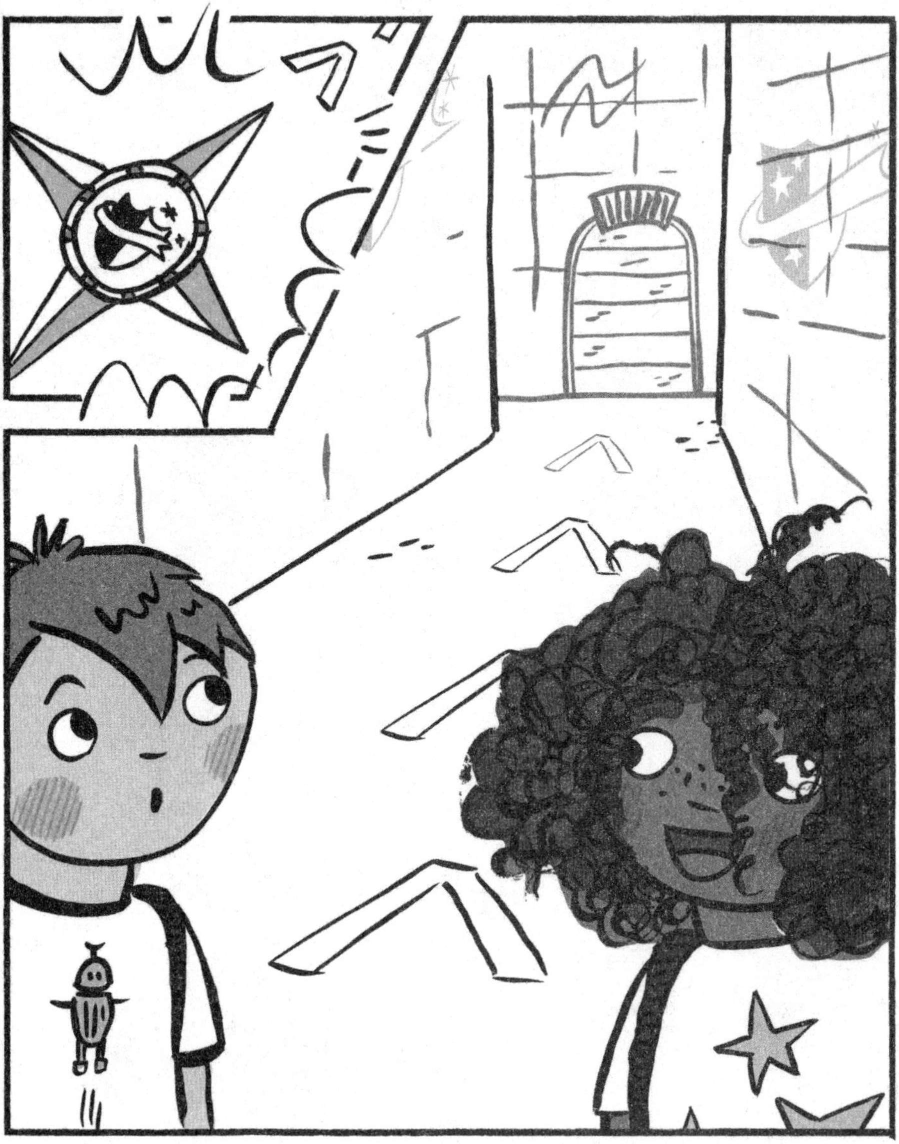

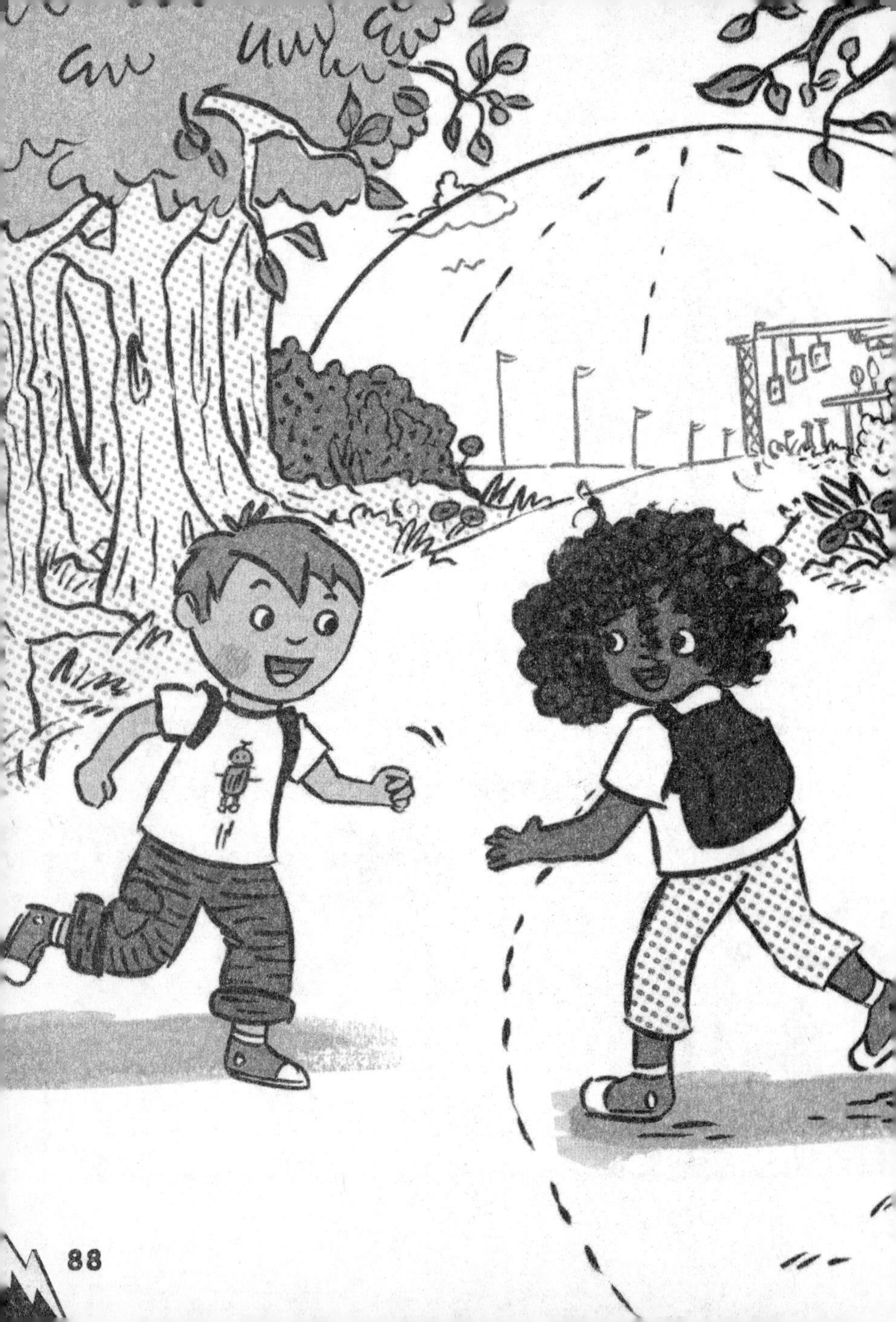

It led straight to the back door.

"Oh, of course—to the Super QT!" I yelled.

As we ran out the door, I explained where we were going.

"There's a huge invisible dome over the racetrack," I said. "Anything that happens inside can't be seen from the outside."

I looked over to make sure Eddie was following me. I could tell from the look on his face that he was excited but really nervous.

When we got to the track, I couldn't believe it! I had expected the place to look like it usually did—a normal infinity racetrack. But today there was a special obstacle course set up!

It was perfect for us! All we needed to do was jump in.

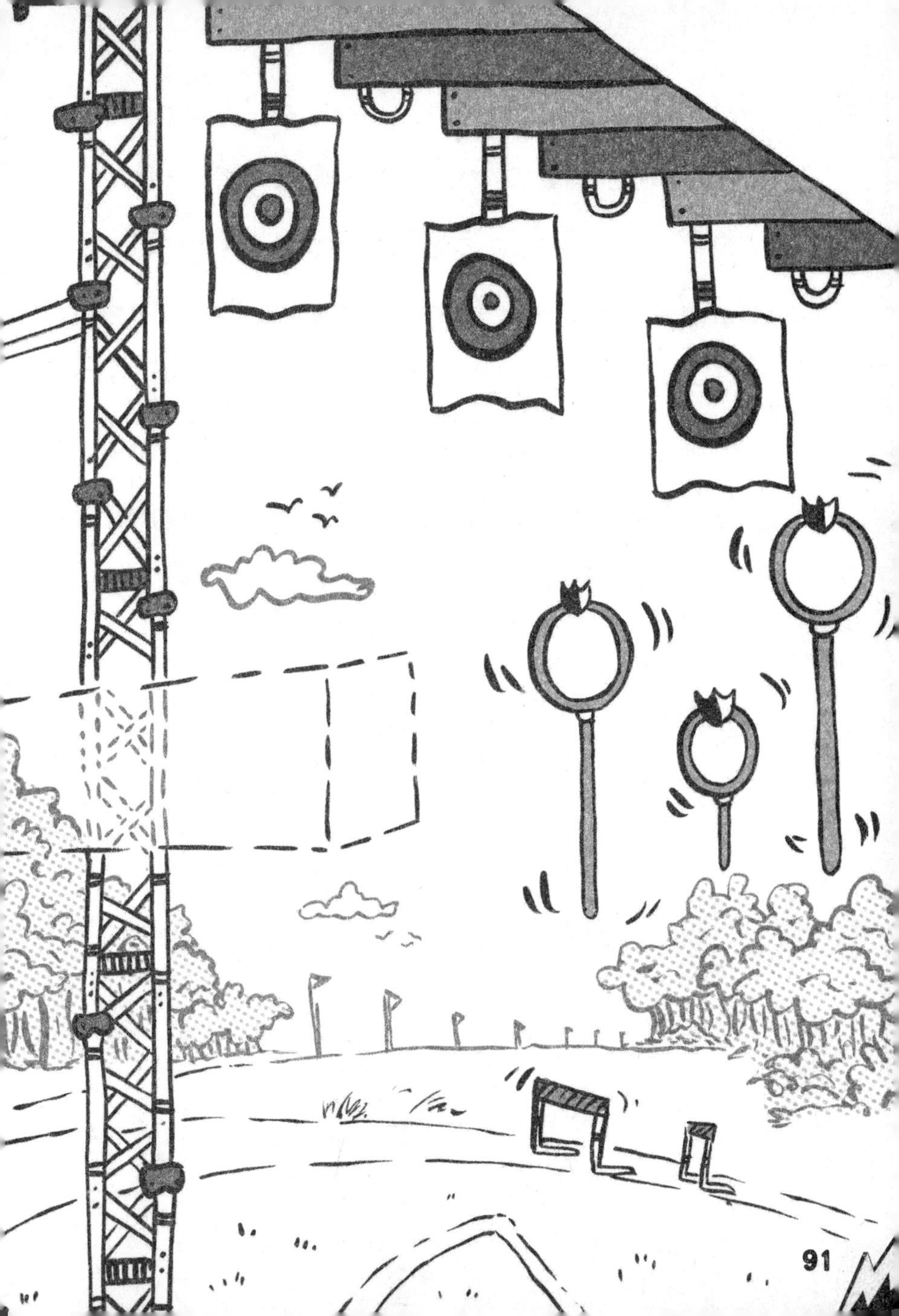

But before that, I needed to teach Eddie one of the basics: how to quick-change into his suit (because let's be real—superheroes don't have time to run to the bathroom). He was really dizzy at first, but soon, with just a spin, he became Eddie Electric!

WHOOSH!

Now he was ready to get on the invisible balance beam. It was a really tricky course, because you had to trust your core balance. Eddie was wobbly and fell off several times. But just as I expected, he didn't give up, and he made it all the way across.

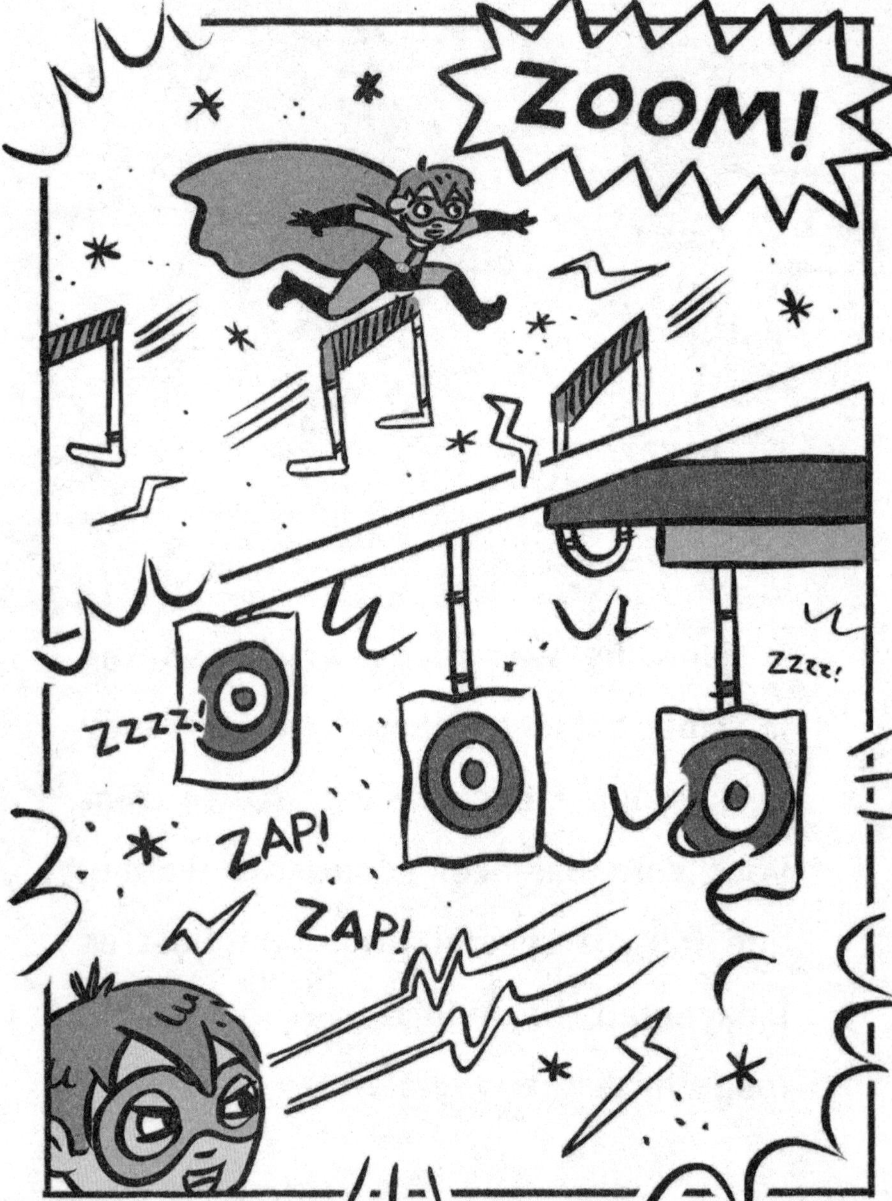
ZOOM!
ZZZZ!
ZZzz!
ZAP!
ZAP!

After that, Eddie practiced his superspeed by jumping over the moving hurdles on the track.

Then it was target practice for his laser powers. There were many close calls along the way, but finally, at the end, it was time to use his superstrength.

"Mia! Is this the right way to hold this?" Eddie asked. He had a gigantic rock on his shoulder. He lifted it with both hands so he could throw it into a moving basket. But as soon as he let go, there was a loud thud as a huge crack ripped through the ground.

"Don't worry, Eddie. Throwing that amount of weight is mega hard!" I yelled, cheering him on from below.

"Wow, this is hard. But you know what?" Eddie asked. "Thank goodness I didn't drop that on my foot!"

We laughed and gave each other a high five as he flew down from the sky.

When we started, neither of us knew how this was going to go.

Sure, there were a few bumps along the way, but one thing was clear: My best friend had a supernatural talent.

HOORAY!

CHAPTER 9

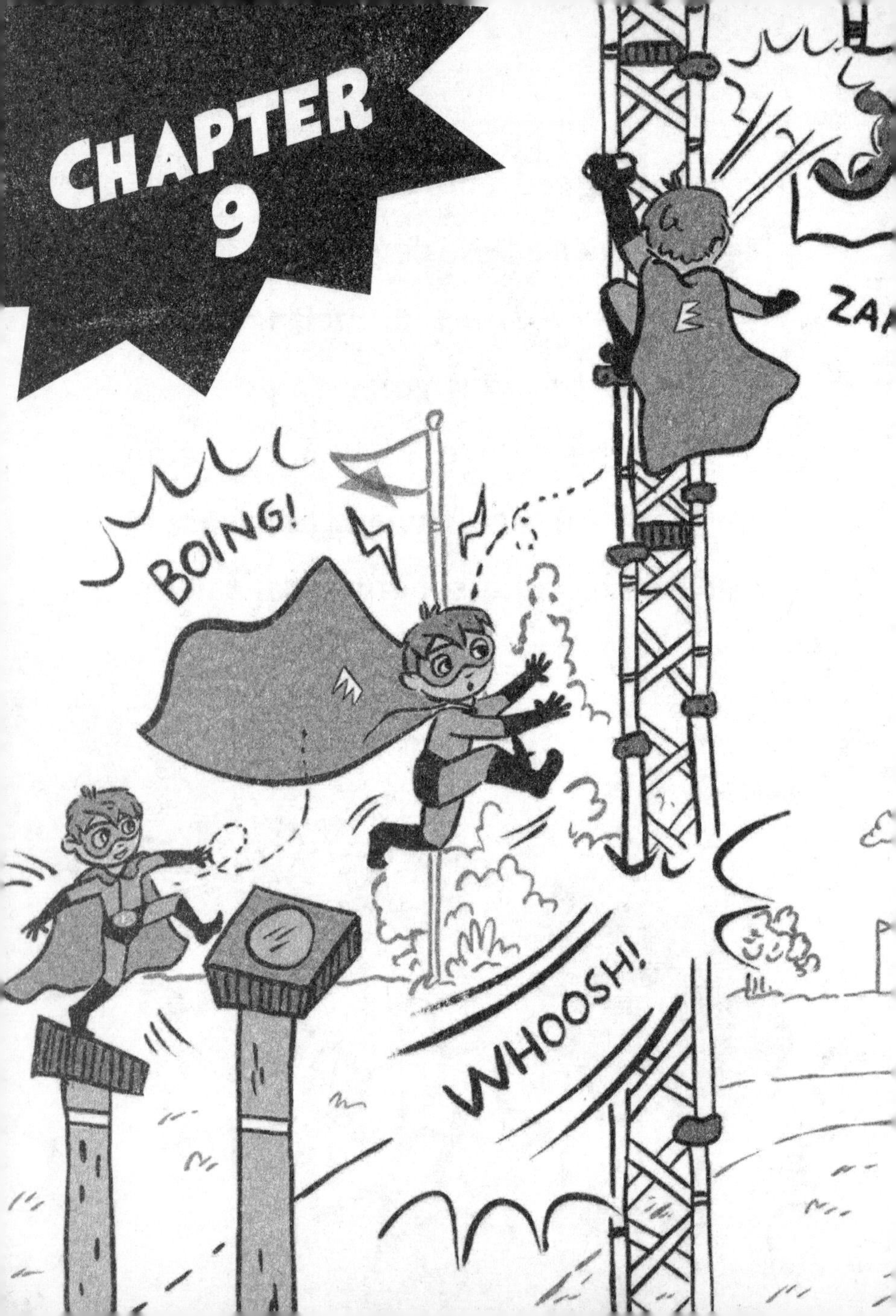
BOING!
WHOOSH!

STILL MIA MAYHEM

After Eddie had practiced each section, I threw in a little twist.

"Okay, let's try running through the whole thing now!"

Eddie smiled big. From the way he burst into the air, I knew he was ready.

He flew up to the invisible beam, and I watched as he skillfully put one foot in front of the other.

I have to admit, it was strange watching him do all kinds of superhero stuff and not be able to join him. I was so used to being part of the action.

But throughout the day, even though I didn't have my powers, I knew I was still me. I mean, we wouldn't have been able to get into the building if I wasn't still Mia Mayhem, right?

GO, EDDIE!

Watching Eddie stumble through some of the hardest exercises made me realize, once again, how important it was to have the right attitude.

Superheroes aren't perfect, but hard work always pays off.

After spending an hour on the course, Eddie was finally able to get through the whole thing. We could have kept going, but one other thing I've learned is that even superheroes need breaks.

So we went back inside, and I gave him a PITS tour. After browsing each floor, we walked through some disco lights into my favorite place.

"Welcome to the student lounge!" I cried.

Eddie's eyes went wide. "You have pinball games? A whole library? And snacks?"

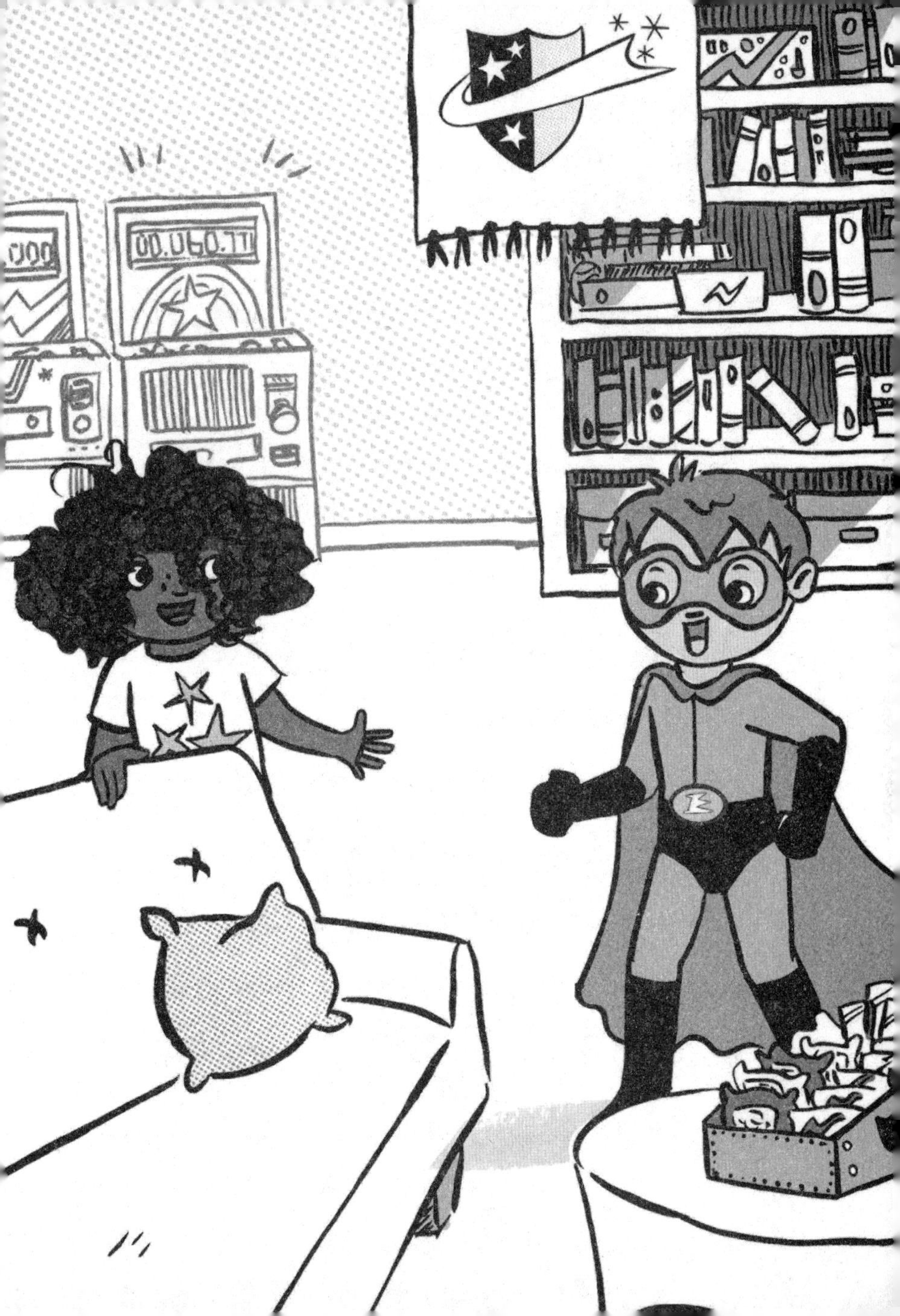

We each grabbed a fizzy water and jumped into a chair.

"Mia, this has been the best day ever," Eddie said. "But now I know . . . this superhero business is so tiring!"

"You bet it is!" I said with a laugh. "But you did awesome today! I'm really proud of you!"

Eddie smiled as I gave him a pat on the back. Then we looked over at the games, and right away, we both knew that the only way to end a great day was to play a totally non-super, fair game . . . of pinball!

After I (happily) lost three times,
Eddie quick-changed
out of his suit, and
we headed back
to the Compass.

Before we
left, Eddie looked
around one last
time.

Then as the secret
exit opened, we saw a very familiar
scene.

A lightning bolt shot down right in front of us.

It was time to get home as fast as we could.

CHAPTER 10

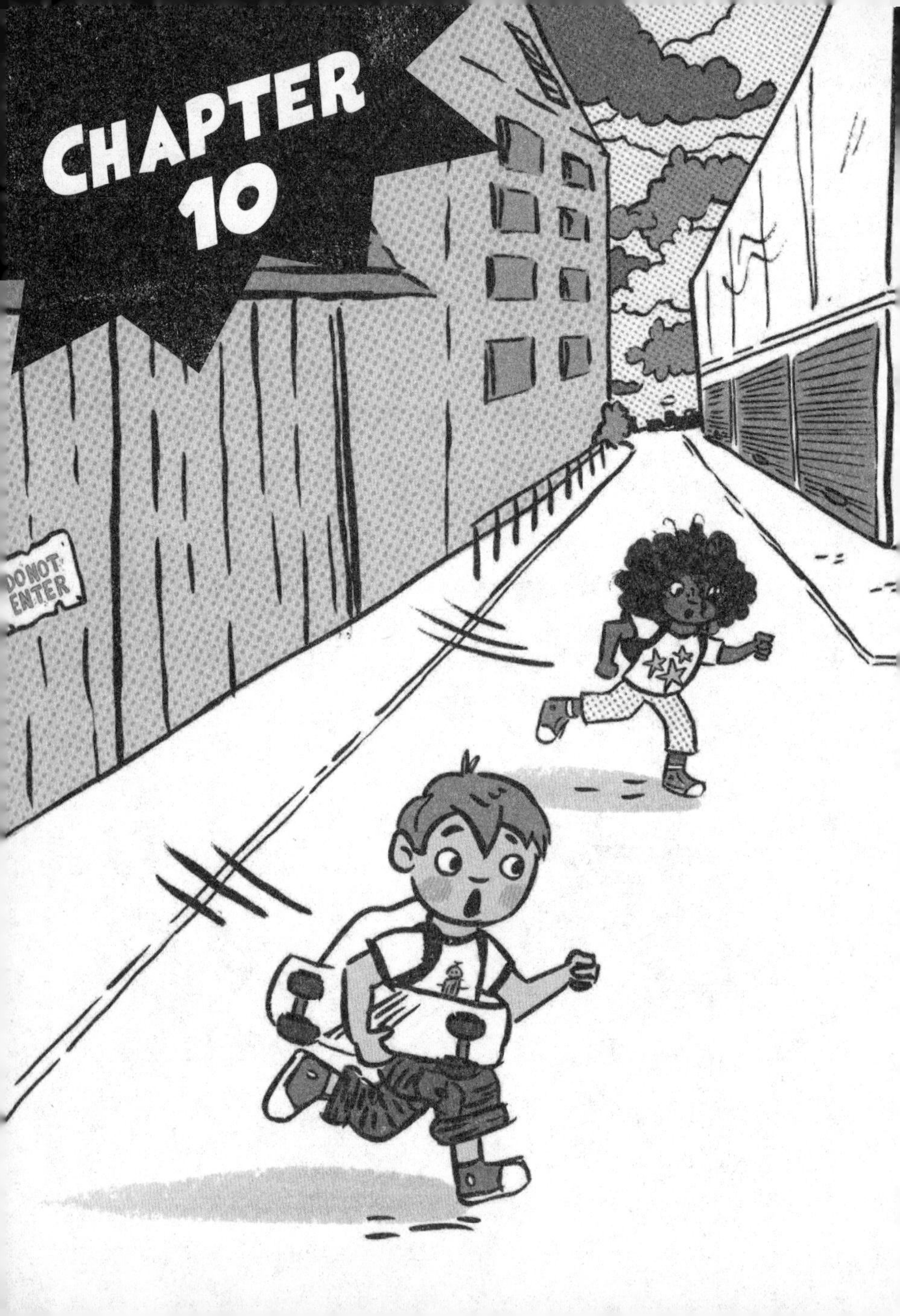
DO NOT ENTER

ANOTHER STORM

Even though Eddie had superspeed, he ran with me and kept my pace. It's something I always knew, but this totally-sideways-yet-totally-normal day reminded me why we were best friends. We stuck with each other, no matter what!

And luckily, we got back to our street before the rain started.

In my driveway, we gave each other a big hug. We had been through some crazy adventures before, but today's was by far the strangest . . . and also my favorite.

Right then, the rain started coming down as another lightning bolt zapped through the sky.

As always, we did our secret handshake. Then, right in the middle of the finger slide, we heard it again.

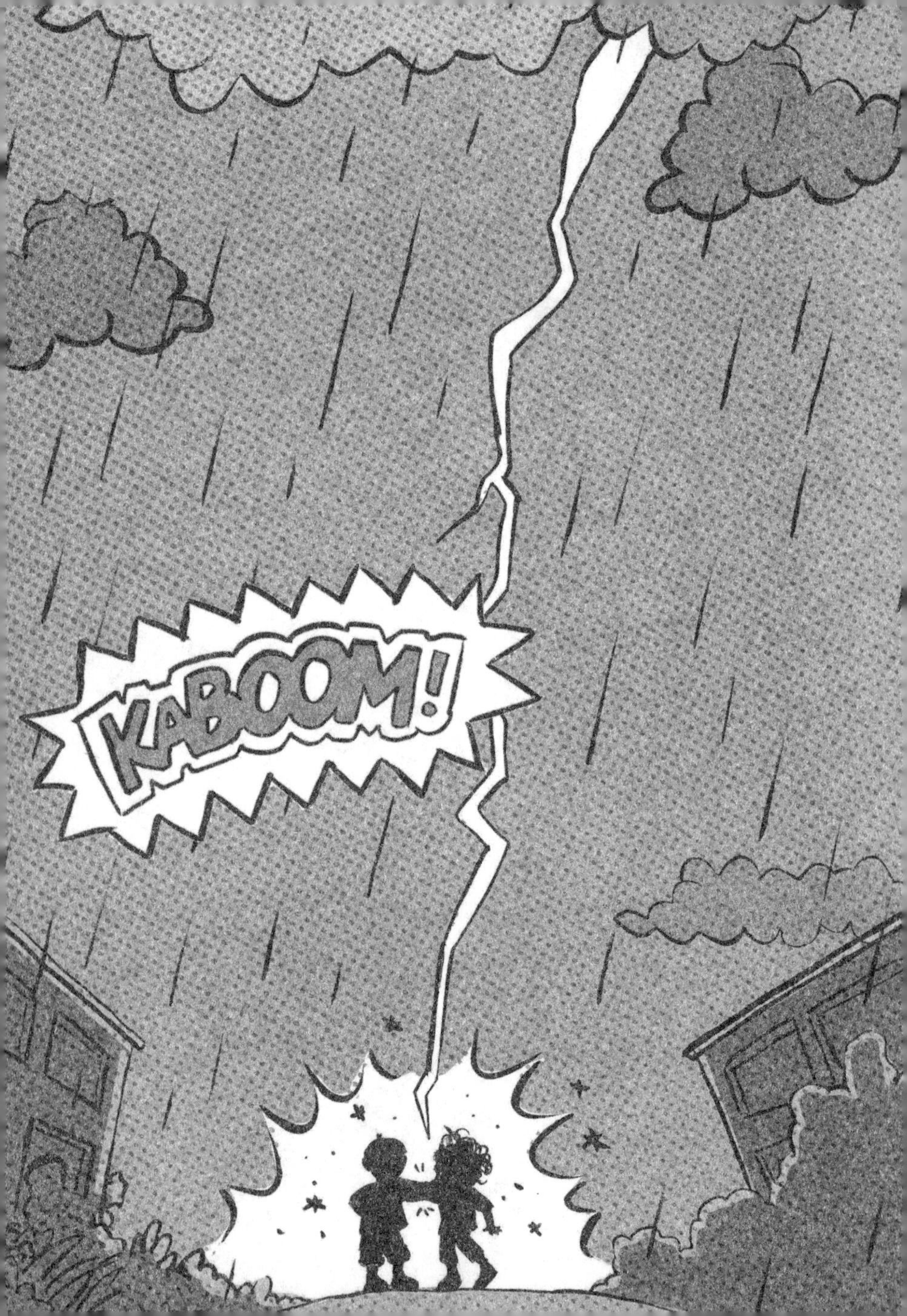
KABOOM!

Another lightning bolt came down, and right away, I felt the same static shock from yesterday. Eddie's eyes met mine, and I knew he felt it too.

I can't explain it, but in that moment, we both knew that everything was going to be okay. Because one superpower we've always shared is reading each other's minds.

We finished our handshake and then ran inside our houses.

I went up to my room to change and found Chaos burrowed under my blankets. After I saw my cat, things felt as normal as ever, right away.

And after another very ordinary dinner (that did include some super-updates for my parents), I was ready to go to sleep.

Today was the first time in a long while that I was literally just Mia Macarooney. I had forgotten how tiring being an eight-year-old could be! As I closed my eyes, for tonight, I was just happy to snuggle with Chaos—whether or not I was a superhero.

When I woke up the next morning, I was excited for a Monday morning to begin!

I brushed my teeth and scarfed down my breakfast . . . all at the speed of light.

Then I packed my books and my supersuit and met Eddie outside.

"Hey, Mia! I've got something for you," he said, handing over a brown paper bag.

On the outside it said: FOR A LITTLE GOOD LUCK.

I opened the
bag and found my
yellow mask.

And that's when
I thought of three
things:

Number one: Yesterday's adventure
was totally *real*.

Number two: Somehow, I was going
to have to explain to Dr. Perb why there
was a huge crack in the Super QT. Wish
me luck.

And number three: Eddie and I
may live in a town called Normal, but
after yesterday, one thing is clear:

There is nothing normal about our thunderstorms.

I don't have answers yet . . . but I have a good feeling that this is a new super-secret that Eddie and I will tackle on the next very rainy day.

DON'T MISS
MIA MAYHEM'S
NEXT ADVENTURE!

"Finally! I found it!" I cheered. I stood on top of my bed, holding my wet suit over my head as if I had just won a trophy.

I emptied every drawer and turned my closet inside out trying to find it. And all this time, it was right on top of my T-shirt pile! I looked around my

Excerpt from *Mia Mayhem Rides the Waves*

room in shock. It looked like a tornado just passed through.

But luckily, it's times like this when being a superhero comes in handy.

Yeah, you heard me right.

My name is Mia Macarooney and *I. Am. A. Superhero!* Like, for real!

My life gets pretty messy sometimes, but no matter how bad things get, I can always clean things up in a flash.

Here, let me show you.

See?

My room looks as good as new, and now finally, I'm one step closer to . . . vacation!

I've been waiting for this day *forever*. I'm so ready that I could burst!

You see, this superhero life gets really busy, really fast.

There's so much to juggle all the time. During the day, my friends and classmates know me as Mia Macarooney. But after regular school ends, I race over to the Program for In Training Superheroes, aka the PITS! The PITS is a top secret superhero training academy where I've learned everything I need to know about being super.

And I wouldn't want things any other way. My life is pretty awesome.

Excerpt from *Mia Mayhem Rides the Waves*